MW01122689

SAVING THE PLANET THROUGH GREEN ENERGY

HYDROPOWER

COLIN GRADY

Enslow Publishing
101 W. 23rd Street
Suite 240
New York, NY 10011
USA

enslow.com

Published in 2017 by Enslow Publishing, LLC.
101 W. 23rd Street, Suite 240, New York, NY 10011

Library of Congress Cataloging-in-Publication Data
Names: Grady, Colin.
Title: Hydropower / Colin Grady.
Description: New York : Enslow Publishing, 2017. | Series: Saving the planet through green energy | Includes bibliographical references and index.
Identifiers: ISBN 9780766082847 (pbk.) | ISBN 9780766082861 (library bound) | ISBN 9780766082854 (6 pack)
Subjects: LCSH: Hydroelectric power plants—Juvenile literature. | Water-power—Juvenile literature.
Classification: LCC TK1081.G68 2017| DDC 621.31'2134—dc23

Printed in China

To Our Readers: We have done our best to make sure all website addresses in this book were active and appropriate when we went to press. However, the author and the publisher have no control over and assume no liability for the material available on those websites or on any websites they may link to. Any comments or suggestions can be sent by e-mail to customerservice@enslow.com.

Portions of this book originally appeared in the book *Hydropower: Making a Splash* by Amy S. Hansen.

Photos Credits: Cover, p. 1 Roman Rybaleov/Shutterstock.com (hydroelectric pumped storage river); Mad Dog/Shutterstock.com (series logo and chapter openers); p. 7 john michael evan potter/Shutterstock.com; p. 9 stockshoppe/Shutterstock.com; p. 10 LacoKozyna/Shutterstock.com; p. 11 Melanie Stetson Freeman/The Christian Science Monitor/Getty Images; p. 14 Songquan Deng/Shutterstock.com; p. 15 John Moore/Getty Images News/Getty Images; p. 17 Sam Hodgson/Bloomberg/Getty Images; p. 19 US Marine Corps/Wikimedia Commons/ USMC-101002-M-4787A-001.jpg/public domain; p. 20 Jeff J Mitchell/Getty Images News/Getty Images; p. 21 FRED TANNEAU/AFP/Getty Images.

CONTENTS

WORDS TO KNOW

atmosphere The gases around an object in space. On Earth, this is air.

bellows A bag with handles that lets out a flow of air when it is opened and closed.

condenses Cools and changes from a gas to a liquid.

endangered species Kinds of animals that will likely die out if people do not keep them safe.

engineers Masters at planning and building engines, machines, roads, and bridges.

environment All the living things and conditions of a place.

generators Machines that make electricity.

gold rush A time in history when people found gold in the ground.

gravity The force that causes objects to move toward each other.

hydroelectric Making electricity from the energy of flowing water.

molecule The smallest bit of matter possible before it can be broken down into its basic parts.

renewable Able to be replaced once it is used up.

turbines Motors that turn by a flow of water or air.

CHAPTER 1

WHAT IS HYDROPOWER?

Have you ever gone rafting on a large river? How about body surfing in the ocean? If so, you know that water can pack a lot of power. Moving water has energy. When we capture and use this energy, we call it hydropower.

In the past, people used hydropower to turn waterwheels. Now we use it to turn **turbines** and to make electricity. To make electricity, the water has to be moving fast. Sometimes we use water flowing over a waterfall. Other times, we build a dam so we can control the water's flow.

Hydropower is a clean, **renewable** energy source. We do not use up the water. We simply borrow its energy.

A dam will hold water behind it until it is released.
The water flow can be used for power.

THE WATER CYCLE

Water is always moving. Every **molecule** of water on Earth is part of the water cycle. This is the pattern of changes that water goes through as it moves across Earth's surface and through the **atmosphere**.

You can see liquid water in rivers, oceans, and puddles. The Sun warms this water. This makes some water molecules evaporate, or turn into a gas called water vapor. As water vapor rises, it cools and **condenses** into clouds. When clouds get heavy, rain or snow falls. Rain and melted snow flow into streams and rivers. The cycle continues, powering turbines around the world.

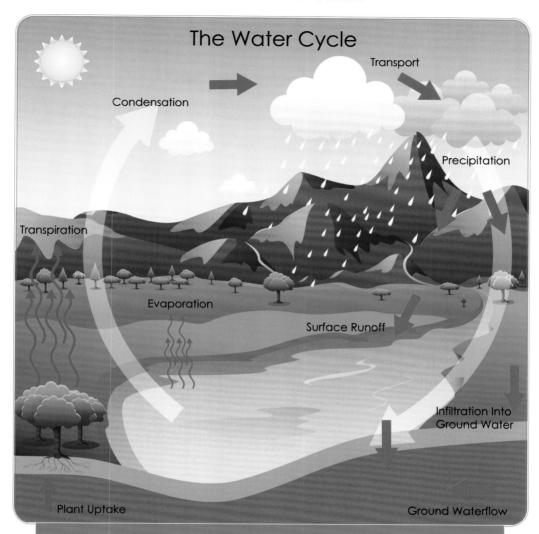

The Water Cycle

Condensation

Transport

Precipitation

Transpiration

Evaporation

Surface Runoff

Infiltration Into Ground Water

Plant Uptake

Ground Waterflow

The water cycle shows how water moves from clouds to land and back to clouds again.

CHAPTER 2

WATER POWER THROUGH HISTORY

A waterwheel was an early way of using water's energy to power a machine. They were used to grind grain and to cut wood.

How long have people been using water's power? Several thousand years ago, people started using waterwheels to capture moving water's energy. Ancient people used waterwheels to do many useful things, such as grinding grain for flour, cutting wood, and operating **bellows** for making iron. In about 65 BCE, a Greek poet even wrote a poem

A waterwheel on the outside of a mill can turn a millstone inside the building. This stone, at a museum in Plymouth, Massachusetts, is grinding corn.

honoring waterwheels! People in ancient India, China, and Syria used waterwheels, too.

Hydropower was important in American history. It powered mills to grind grain and weave cloth. In 1880, people made electricity using a water turbine for the first time in Grand Rapids, Michigan.

HYDROPOWER TIMELINE

200   Waterwheels are used in China to make strong iron.

1877   Lester Pelton invents a new kind of water turbine. It is used to run machines during the California **gold rush**.

1882   Appleton, Wisconsin, becomes the first city in the United States to use hydroelectricity.

1936   The Hoover Dam starts producing electricity.

1967   The new La Rance Tidal Barrage starts producing electricity on the Rance River in Brittany, France.

1978   The US Supreme Court rules that dams cannot flood the homes of **endangered species**. Construction on the Tellico Dam in Tennessee is held up and a fish called the snail darter is moved.

1982   A tidal energy system opens at the Bay of Fundy, in Nova Scotia, Canada. It produces enough electricity for 6,000 homes.

2008   The Portuguese put a system known as the sea serpent into the ocean to collect wave energy for electricity. It is removed in March 2009 to fix problems.

2009   Scientists use wave power to move tools around the ocean so that they can listen to whales.

2012   The United States is fourth in the world in making hydroelectric power, after China, Brazil, and Canada. The Columbia River basin in Washington makes 44 percent of the hydroelectricity for the United States.

2012   The Three Gorges Dam in China becomes the largest hydroelectric dam in the world.

2016   Hydroelectric power is the largest source of renewable power in the United States. It makes more than 6 percent of the country's electricity.

CHAPTER 3

USING WATER TO MAKE ELECTRICITY

You can imagine the power of the water that gushes over Niagara Falls.

A **hydroelectric** plant is a power station that uses the energy in moving water to make electricity. Most of these plants are built along big rivers. For example, the Niagara River, in Ontario, Canada, and New York, supplies lots of electricity. Every second, more than 530,000 gallons (2 million liters) of water shoot over Niagara Falls, dropping 167 feet (51 meters). Upstream and downstream, hydroelectric plants produce electricity.

If a river does not have a waterfall, **engineers** may build a dam. The dam holds back a river's water and forms a body of water called a reservoir or a lake behind the dam.

Water goes through a dam along the Niagara River in New York. A power plant uses the water's energy to make electricity.

Dam operators let water out through pipes in the dam walls. The falling water spins turbines. These turbines turn **generators** that make electricity.

LAKE MEAD AND THE HOOVER DAM

The Hoover Dam, on the Colorado River between Colorado and Nevada, has a huge hydroelectric plant. This big dam is 726 feet (221 meters) tall. When the dam was first built, the Colorado River filled up the reservoir, called Lake Mead. Lake Mead is 110 miles (177 kilometers) long.

To get electricity, engineers let water from Lake Mead flow into pipes. The water falls, spinning turbines that make electricity. The water then continues down the Colorado River. The Hoover Dam produces enough electricity to power a city of 750,000 people. The electricity goes to Arizona, California, and Nevada.

Water from the Hoover Dam spins these turbines to make electricity.

CHAPTER 4
WATER WAVES FOR ENERGY

Whenever the wind pushes on water, waves are formed. Waves are another form of water energy. Some engineers use these water waves to make electricity. One way is to build channels that force waves together. The waves get more powerful and can turn turbines, which generate electricity.

Another system uses buoys, or floats, with special pumps inside. The buoys change the bobbing energy of the waves into electricity. The electricity travels to the shore through wires running along the ocean floor. The US Marine Corp set up buoys in Hawaii to supply power for a base.

ENERGY FROM THE TIDES

Scientists have also found ways to make electricity from the tides. Tides are changes in water level, at the seashore and in tidal rivers, that happen several times a day. They are created by the tug of the moon's **gravity** on the oceans.

In France, people make electricity using a barrage, or small dam. When the tide comes

A large buoy that floats off the coast of Hawaii turns energy from the waves into electrical power.

When placed in the water, this large tidal energy turbine will act like an underwater windmill. The moving water, due to the tides, will turn the turbines to make electricity.

in, water is caught in the dam. The water then goes out slowly, spinning turbines on its way. This system produces enough power for 200,000 homes.

Engineers in the Philippines are planning a tidal fence. It would use a line of underwater turbines to produce electricity from the rising and falling tides.

CHAPTER 5

STILL THINGS TO THINK ABOUT

Is hydroelectric power safe for the **environment**? After all, the power is clean and renewable. Yet, it can still hurt the environment. Building big dams floods large areas with water. These places were once home to plants, animals, and, sometimes, people. In some cases, the dams mean millions of people have to leave when their town gets flooded with water upstream of the dam.

Tidal farms will have turbines in the water, like the one shown here, that are connected to a power grid on land that makes electricity.

Dams also make it hard for fish to move. Some hydroelectric plants build fish ladders, which help fish move past the dam. Dams can also cause mudslides. If the new lake is put in a spot that cannot hold up the water's weight, ground at the lake's edges can cave in.

HYDROPOWER AND THE FUTURE

Most of Earth is covered with water, so scientists will keep finding new ways to capture its energy. Small dams are one idea. They cause fewer environmental problems than large dams. There are also tiny hydroelectric systems that villages use to produce a little electricity.

Engineers want to capture the energy in small waves, too. One system uses a water-filled tube called the Anaconda. When the water ripples, a bulge forms, moves down the tube, and spins a turbine. The turbine powers a generator. Who knows what the next form of hydropower will be?

FURTHER READING

BOOKS

Centore, Michael. *Renewable Energy.* Broomall, PA: Mason Crest, 2015.

Dickmann, Nancy. *Energy from Water: Hydroelectric, Tidal, and Wave Power.* New York, NY: Crabtree Publishing Co., 2016.

Kopp, Megan. *Living in a Sustainable Way: Green Communities.* New York, NY: Crabtree Publishing Co., 2016.

Otfinoski, Steven. *Wind, Solar, and Geothermal Power: From Concept to Consumer.* New York, NY: Children's Press, 2016.

Sneideman, Joshua. *Renewable Energy: Discover the Fuel of the Future with 20 Projects.* White River Junction, VT: Nomad Press, 2016.

Spilsbury, Richard. *Energy.* Chicago, IL: Capstone Press, 2014.

WEBSITES

Energy Star Kids
energystar.gov/index.cfm?c=kids.kids_index
Learn more facts about energy, how you can save energy, and how to help the planet.

NASA's Climate Kids: Energy
climatekids.nasa.gov/menu/energy
Lots of fun facts and links about energy.

US Energy Information Administration
eia.gov/kids
Read about the history of energy, get facts about the types of energy, learn tips to save energy, and link to games and activities.

INDEX